A NEW HOPE™

DK

LONDON, NEW YORK, MUNICH,
MELBOURNE and DELHI

Editor Emma Grange
Designer Jon Hall
Senior Pre-Production Producer Jennifer Murray
Producer Louise Minihane
Managing Editor Elizabeth Dowsett
Design Manager Ron Stobbart
Publishing Manager Julie Ferris
Art Director Lisa Lanzarini
Publishing Director Simon Beecroft

Designed for DK by Sandra Perry

Reading Consultant
Maureen Fernandes

Dorling Kindersley would like to thank: Randi Sørensen and
Robert Stefan Ekblom at the LEGO Group and J. W. Rinzler,
Leland Chee, Troy Alders and Carol Roeder at Lucasfilm.

First published in Great Britain in 2014 by
Dorling Kindersley Limited
80 Strand, London, WC2R 0RL

10 9 8 7 6 5 4
010–195510–July/14

Page design copyright © 2014 Dorling Kindersley Limited

LEGO, the LEGO logo, the Brick and Knob configurations
and the Minifigure are trademarks of the LEGO Group.
© 2014 The LEGO Group
Produced by Dorling Kindersley Limited under licence
from the LEGO Group.

© 2014 Lucasfilm Ltd. & ™. All rights reserved.
Used under authorisation.

A CIP catalogue record for this book
is available from the British Library.

ISBN: 978-1-40934-968-6

Colour reproduction in the UK by Altaimage
Printed and bound in China

Discover more at
www.dk.com
www.starwars.com
www.LEGO.com/starwars

Contents

A NEW HOPE™

Written by Emma Grange

Welcome to Tatooine
Meet Luke Skywalker.

macrobinoculars

Luke lives a quiet life with
his uncle Owen on their farm
on the sandy planet Tatooine.

Luke doesn't know it yet,
but his life is about to change
forever…

Uncle Owen

War in the galaxy

The man in the scary black suit is Darth Vader.

He commands an army of soldiers called stormtroopers.

Darth Vader's evil Empire has seized control of the galaxy.

Stormtrooper

The Empire has
built a powerful
weapon called
the Death Star.

Death Star

Who can stop the Empire?

Darth Vader

Meet the rebels

The rebels are a group of people who want to free the galaxy from the Empire.

Some rebels have stolen the plans to the Death Star.

The plans show them that the Death Star has a weak spot.

Now they can destroy it!

A brave rebel called
Princess Leia is determined
to defeat the Empire.

Rebel
soldier

Princess Leia

Vader's prisoner

Where is Princess Leia now?

She has been taken
prisoner by Darth Vader!

Darth Vader wants her
to return the plans to the
Death Star.

Prison
cell

Droids to the rescue!

This is Princess Leia's faithful droid R2-D2.

Princess Leia hopes R2-D2 can find a man called Obi-Wan Kenobi.

Obi-Wan will help the rebels fight the Empire.

R2-D2 and
another droid
called C-3PO flee
in an escape pod to
the planet Tatooine.

droid

Good luck, droids!

escape pod

C-3PO

On Tatooine again

Here is Luke Skywalker
again.

His uncle Owen needs
to buy droids to work
on his farm.

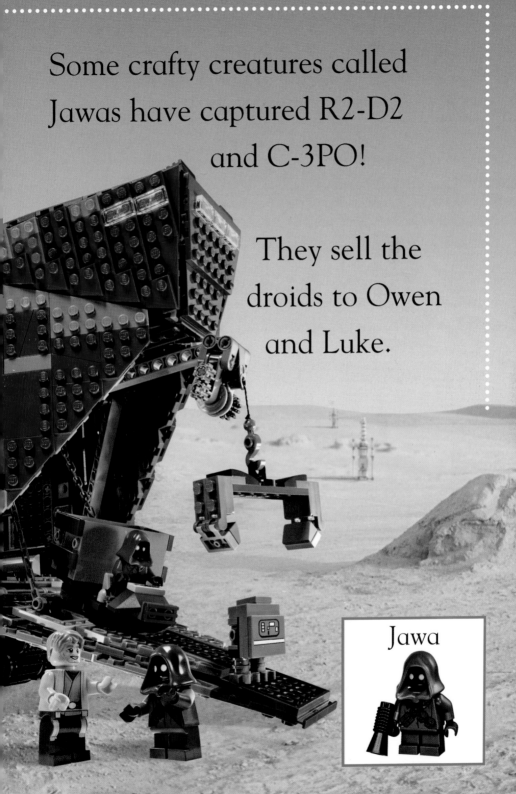

Some crafty creatures called Jawas have captured R2-D2 and C-3PO!

They sell the droids to Owen and Luke.

Jawa

Hidden Jedi

Luke's friend Ben Kenobi
has a secret.

He is actually the Jedi Master
Obi-Wan Kenobi!

Jedi

R2-D2 gives Obi-Wan a
message from Princess Leia.

Obi-Wan will try to help her.

Obi-Wan tells Luke that he
could learn to be a Jedi, too,
but Luke must leave Tatooine
and help fight the Empire.

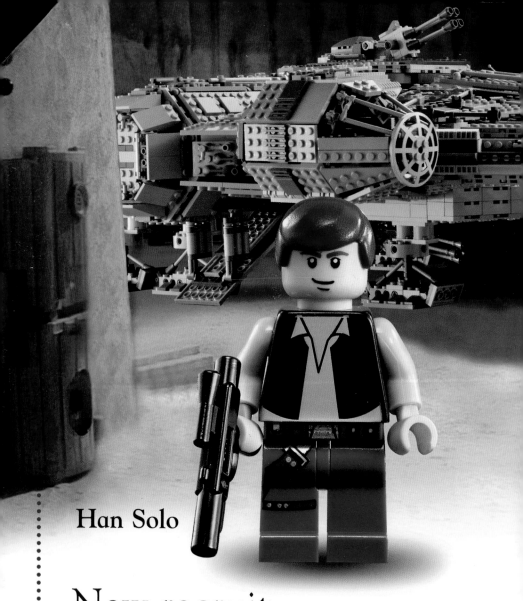

Han Solo

New recruit

Luke, Obi-Wan, R2-D2 and
C-3PO need a ship to take
them to rescue Princess Leia.

Millennium Falcon

Maybe this
man could help?

His name is Han Solo
and he has a ship called
the *Millennium Falcon.*

Obi-Wan promises Han
a great reward if he helps
them to rescue the princess.

Rescue operation

Is that two stormtroopers approaching?

No, it is Luke Skywalker and Han Solo in disguise!

Luke and Han rescue
Princess Leia, but then they
fall into a waste disposal unit.

Luckily, R2-D2 and
C-3PO are on hand
to save them.

That was
close!

A great sacrifice

Obi-Wan Kenobi is a very
brave Jedi Master.

Obi-Wan distracts Darth
Vader so that his friends
can escape unnoticed.

In a fearsome one-on-one lightsaber battle, Darth Vader defeats the old Jedi Master.

Lightsaber

X-wing

Space battle

The time has come for
the rebels to put their
plan into action.

The rebels fly X-wings when attacking the Death Star, with the Empire's forces trying to blast them in their TIE fighters.

The fast and furious battle takes place deep in space.

TIE fighter

Death Star destroyed

Luke Skywalker is an excellent pilot.

He flies his X-wing close to the Death Star, avoiding all the TIE fighters.

Then he fires a shot at just the right spot to make the Death Star explode.

The Death Star is destroyed! Well done, Luke!

Celebration

The rebels have faced many challenges.

They have lost some old friends, but have also made new ones along the way.

Princess Leia gives medals
to the brave rebels as a reward
for their courage.

The Death Star weapon is
destroyed, but the fight against
the Empire is not over yet...

Glossary

Death Star
A weapon as large as a moon, capable of destroying whole planets.

Droid
A metal robot programmed to help and obey its owner.

Jawa
Creatures that live on Tatooine and collect materials to sell to people.

Jedi
A warrior who uses the Force for good and to protect the galaxy.

Lightsaber
A weapon of pure energy, used by the Jedi and others in battle.

Index

Here are some other DK books you might enjoy.

Star Wars™ Are Ewoks Scared of Stormtroopers?
Meet the bravest heroes in the *Star Wars* galaxy,
who defeat evil villains against all odds.

Angry Birds™ *Star Wars*™ Darth Swindle's Secrets
Wicked Darth Swindle has many secrets! Learn
all about this sly swine and his pesky pals.

LEGO® *Star Wars*™ The Phantom Menace™
Who has brought the LEGO® *Star Wars*® galaxy
to the brink of war? Can the Jedi stop them?

LEGO® *Star Wars*™ Attack of the Clones™
Meet evil Count Dooku! Can the Republic's
clone troopers defeat the Sith's droid army?

LEGO® *Star Wars*™ The Empire Strikes Back™
The galaxy is at war. Can the brave rebels rise up to defeat
the evil Emperor and his apprentice Darth Vader?

LEGO® Legends of Chima™: Tribes of Chima
Friend or Foe? Meet the amazing animal tribes of Chima
and discover their fearsome vehicles and weapons.